Rodney Peppé

THE MICE ON THE MOON

A Doubleday Book for Young Readers

Also by Rodney Peppé

HERE COMES HUXLEY PIG

HUXLEY PIG THE CLOWN

HUXLEY PIG'S AIRPLANE

HUXLEY PIG'S MODEL CAR

THUMBPRINT CIRCUS

A Doubleday Book for Young Readers

Published by
Delacorte Press
Bantam Doubleday Dell Publishing Group, Inc.
666 Fifth Avenue
New York, New York 10103

Doubleday and the portrayal of an anchor with a dolphin are trademarks of Bantam Doubleday Dell Publishing Group, Inc.

This work was originally published in Great Britain in 1992 by Penguin Books Ltd.

Library of Congress Cataloging in Publication Data

Peppé, Rodney.

The mice on the moon/Rodney Peppé.

p. cm.

Summary: The mouse family builds a spaceship out of an egg carton and sets off for the moon, little realizing that they have an unwelcome passenger along on the trip.

ISBN: 0=385=30839=6

[1. Mice–Fiction. 2. Space flight to the moon–Fiction. 3.Moon–Fiction.] I. Title.

PZ7.P4212Mh 1993

[E]–dc20
                                                        92-5212
                                                          CIP
                                                           AC

Manufactured in China

August 1993

10 9 8 7 6 5 4 3 2 1

ISBN-0 385 30839 6

Pip and his brothers and sisters found the
biggest firework they had ever seen.
"It's dangerous!" said Pip.
"Yes!" said Sue. "We mustn't touch it!"

So they hurried home to the shoe house to tell the grown-ups all about it.

The family went to see the giant rocket.
"Look!" said Pa. "The blue fuse hasn't
even been lit. You were right not to touch it,
children."
Grandpa observed, "On a good day, it might
just reach the moon!"

That night at storytime, Pip asked Grandpa,
"Could we really fly to the moon in that rocket?"
And Grandpa replied, "We'd never get back
to Earth!"
"We could," persisted Pip, "if we built
a spaceship!"

"For a little mouse that's a very big idea!"
said Grandpa.

The next day Pip and his brothers and sisters went to D. Rat, the junk dealer, to find a strong, empty carton.

"Don't mess up my egg boxes," he snapped.

"I like to keep 'em tidy!"

Pip paid for the empty carton.
"And what are you going to do with that?"
inquired D. Rat, suspiciously.
"It's a surprise," said Pip.

D. Rat didn't like surprises.

"It's a wonderful egg box," said Ma.
"It will make a fine spaceship," said Grandpa.

"Of course!" said Ma. "Why didn't I think of that?"

Pip explained to the family his idea of flying
to the moon in an egg box. And to offer
encouragement, Grandpa said, with a wink,

"Everyone knows the moon is made of cheese."
So they all set to work making a spaceship.
But nobody noticed D. Rat watching them.

When the spaceship was finished, they took it to the launch pad. And who should be inspecting the rocket but D. Rat. "How clever you've been with my egg box!" he observed. "Flying to the moon, are we?"

Though the mice couldn't understand why,
D. Rat was most helpful. Almost too helpful!
"Let me lend you a paw," he said, tying their
spaceship to the rocket. He even offered to
light the fuse!

"IGNITION!" screamed D. Rat. "Five, four, three, two, one, LIFT-OFF!"

The rocket fired, and moved slowly upwards . . .

. . . faster and faster, up, up high in the sky!

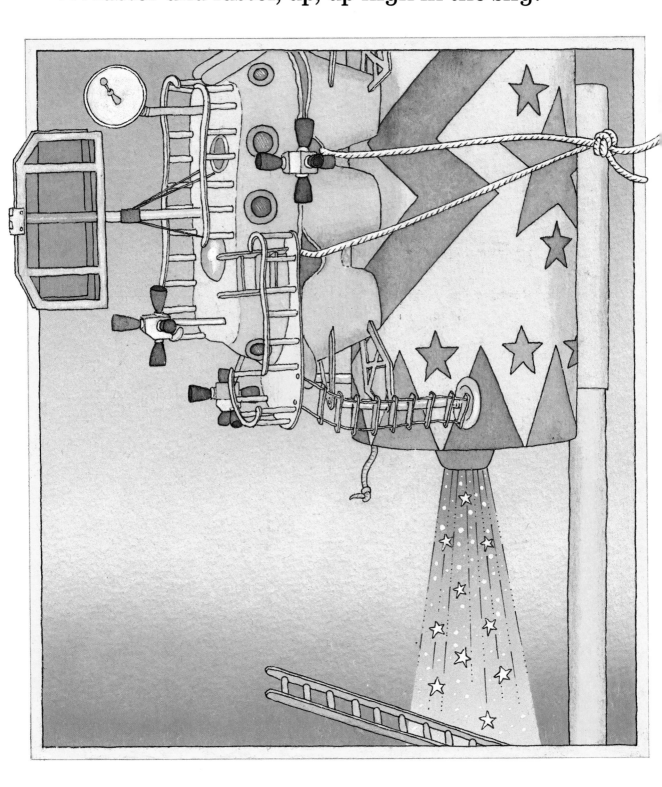

Soon the mice were on their way to the moon.
"Now is the time to cut the string," said Grandpa.
And they separated from the rocket.

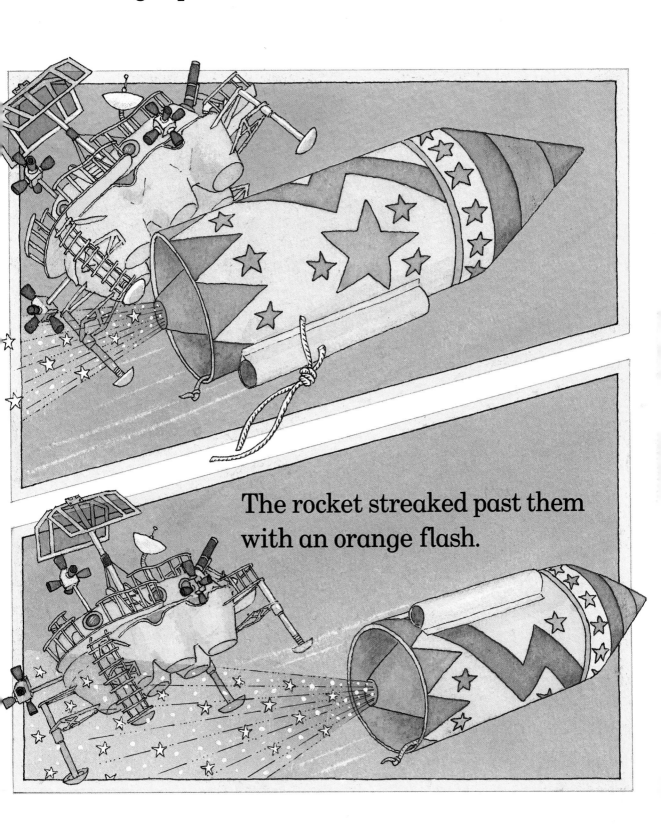

The rocket streaked past them
with an orange flash.

At last the mice were in outer space.
They came out on deck to look back at Earth.

That is, all except Grandma, who was driving.

"I'll turn on the landing motors," said Grandma. "We're going to land on the moon."

The surface was full of holes.
It looked just like a huge, round cheese!

"Pip!" called Grandpa. "You must be the first mouse on the moon." So Pip climbed down and stepped onto the surface. "That's one small step for a mouse," said Pa.

"And one giant leap for mousekind!" said Ma.

The first thing Pip did was to dig into the surface with his shovel. "That's not cheese, Grandpa!" he cried.

"Dear me!" said Grandpa. "I must have been misinformed!"

But the children were far too excited to worry about the cheese. Soon they were leaping about like kangaroos!

They weighed so much less on the moon, giant leaps were easy.

"Wheeeeeeee!" went Pip, as he sailed over a rock.
"Come on. Let's explore the moon!"
Ma said, "Don't stray too far from the spaceship,"
as the others followed Pip.

But with such giant leaps, the children were soon far away. They gathered around some rocks and couldn't believe their eyes.
There, in a crater, was the crashed rocket!

"Aha, little mice!" came a familiar voice.
"I hitched a ride on your rocket and got here
first! The moon is mine . . . and all the cheese!"
"There isn't any cheese, D. Rat," said Pip.
"Rubbish! Everyone knows the moon is made of
cheese," argued D. Rat, echoing Grandpa's words.

D. Rat patted his pockets, which were full of gunpowder from the rocket. "Start digging," he ordered, "or I'll blow up your spaceship!" So Pip began to dig until he got tired. "Keep going!" snarled D. Rat. "You'll soon get through to the cheese."

But Grandpa came to the rescue.
"No profit in that, D. Rat," he called from the
rocks. "You can't get back to Earth without the
spaceship!"

"Drat!" said D. Rat. "I hadn't thought of that!"
He kicked at a rock, and then brightened.
"Does that mean," he wheedled, "that you have
room for one more aboard?"

The spaceship slowly lifted off the surface of the moon. And it began its journey back to Earth.

The mice were safely inside, but D. Rat had to take his chance outside.

As the mice floated to Earth, with D. Rat a little singed, Ma said, "It was lucky I made the parachutes!" "We'll soon be home!" shouted Grandpa.

"Ah!" sighed Pip. "Cheese…at last!"